SASSY PANTS

SASSY PANTS

written by Carol Brown

An *almost* true story based *very* loosely on *some* facts.

TATE PUBLISHING & *Enterprises*

Sassy Pants

Published by Tate Publishing & Enterprises, LLC
127 E. Trade Center Terrace | Mustang, Oklahoma 73064 USA
1.888.361.9473 | www.tatepublishing.com

Tate Publishing is committed to excellence in the publishing industry. The company reflects the philosophy established by the founders, based on Psalm 68:11,
"The Lord gave the word and great was the company of those who published it."

Cover & interior design by Lindsay B. Behrens
Illustration by Liz Holt

Published in the United States of America

ISBN: 978-1-61663-841-2
1. Juvenile Fiction / Animals / Farm Animals
2. Juvenile Fiction / Social Issues / Manners & Etiquette
10.08.03

Dedicated to my granddaughter, Kathrine,
whose favorite friend is "Pig!"

TABLE OF CONTENTS

PROLOGUE

An interesting thing happened every spring on a woodsy little farm backed right up to the state forest, tucked away in the hills of northeastern Iowa, not very far from the old Mississippi River. Most of the state is flat like a pancake, but this farm was in the one spot the glacier missed when it slid off the North Pole and flattened everything in its way! Here, in this part of the state, it left hills and valleys, little creeks and rivers. Farmer White said the farm would have been much larger if it was not standing on end! It was a delightful farm—a treasure chest waiting to be discovered! Arrowheads left by Indians were everywhere, just under the surface of the ground. A log cabin built of huge old logs by Irish settlers still stood on the "back eighty." Every now and then one of the boys found a barrel hoop that held a whiskey barrel together from the time when alcohol was illegal! The hoops were rusty, but shined right up and made wonderful toys! If you had a good imagination you could be an Indian kid, or an Irish settler, or a "bootlegger" hiding from the G-men! Oh, I am rambling! Back to why we are here!

Each spring all the new animals gathered around the water trough—the new little pigs, sheep, kittens, chickens, ducks, and so on, as well as any new grownup animals that Farmer White brought to the farm.

Spring weather turned the barnyard talk to Sassy Pants. Excitement started to build in the air. Some of the older residents came to the Spring Story Fest as well; it was a wonderful time of remembering! Older animals smiled when asked questions about her. Some shuddered at the memory of those days.

Miss Molly Merino, of the Merino herd, was the barnyard instructor. Her family was well known for producing the finest, softest, most fluffy wool of any sheep! Mrs. White knit many a soft sweater to warm little backs from that wool! Miss Molly taught all the new arrivals the manners and rules of the farm by telling Sassy Pants's story—a most delightful way to learn! Molly was a wee bit of a lamb herself when it all happened—some of it happened to Miss Molly herself, so she remembers it well!

Oh, I see Molly is patting her head, looking for her glasses—she's about to begin! Look she is rapping her hoof on the water trough to get everyone's attention. Let's listen in!

"Children, children, give me your eyes! You little ones there in front find a comfortable spot." The children stopped talking and wiggled and squirmed to find their spot. "Adults, you move in there around the back! There! That's better! Okay children, are we ready? Listen carefully to the tale I'm about to tell, for there is much to learn!" Everyone quieted as Miss Molly adjusted her glasses and leaned forward. "Here is how it all happened!"

SASSY PANTS

"To anyone walking by, Sassy Pants was an ordinary pig. She rooted with her snout and rolled in the mud. She smacked as she ate smelly things from the trough—pig soup, Farmer White called it. He poured whey in a big barrel, added three-days-old potato and carrot peelings, table scraps that Mrs. White saved for a week, rotten cabbage and onions that died in the cellar before spring, old corn covered with mildew, and leftover oats. Then he flavored it with whey from the creamery or soured milk, stirred it all up,

and poured it in the trough. Pigs are very fond of Farmer White's "soup." I am sure you will like it," Miss Molly said to the little piggies in the front row. "However, when I took a sniff, the smell made me dizzy in the head! Sassy Pants smacked it down with all the other pigs. But it was not always that way!

"No, she did not start out an ordinary pig. If you were to ask Mrs. White, the farmer's wife, she would tell you Sassy Pants was no ordinary pig! Au contraire! No, she was trouble! She was so much trouble that Mrs. White wanted to shorten her tail—right up next to her ears!

'"Oh, my! That is a bit short!' you say! Well, Mrs. White had her reasons, I assure you.

"It began when Sassy Pants was a little oinker. She was sandy of color and smallish in size, with a pink curly tail and beady little eyes. She was the last of the litter of nineteen piglets, and, I am sorry to say, the smallest. Being the smallest of the lot, Sassy Pants had a difficult time getting enough to eat! The problem was that Mrs. Pig had nineteen piggies but only eighteen place settings! There was not enough to go around. The larger piggies hogged it all and pushed little Sassy Pants into a corner. But Sassy Pants did not take that lying down. No sir-ee! She squealed; she pushed and shoved. She climbed on top of the others to steal their plates. She made a ruckus. She was determined, you see, determined to get what was hers…well, what she *thought* was hers.

"Farmer White heard the noise in the pig barn and came right over. Immediately he saw what the problem was. Scooping up the hungry little piggy, he brought her to the house for Mrs. White to feed. That, my friends, is when and where the trouble started."

LIFE IN THE BIG HOUSE

"In the big house, Mrs. White held the squirming little piggy, admiring her pink, curly, little tail and her blue, blue eyes. 'Poor little thing,' she said. 'Did those other piggies not let you have anything to eat?' From the cupboard came the piggy bottle. Mrs. White filled it with milk, and Sassy Pants ate 'til she thought she would pop. Her eyes became heavy, and she fell asleep, snuggled in a blanket in a box in an out-of-the-way corner behind the kitchen stove, dreaming little piggy sorts of dreams.

"When she awoke, she saw the faces of three little boys peering at her over the top of her box. Mrs. White had four boys, but Denny, the oldest boy, was not particularly fond of pigs—but that is another story. It was lunchtime! The boys thought it great fun to hold little Sassy Pants to feed her. She made cute, contented grunting sounds when she ate. Day after day, she gobbled her food and slept in her box. In no time she was big enough to eat table scraps—all the things little boys did not want to eat.

"No longer content to stay in her box, she tipped it over and went for a walk—in the house! She walked across the room and down the hall into the bathroom, where she tipped over the trash. She did not notice, nor did she care about the mess she made.

She wrapped herself in toilet paper and went to look for Mrs. White, who was busy making supper. A hard little nose rubbed on her socks. 'Oh! Oh! Oh! How did you get out? Look at you, you naughty little pig. Are you going to be trouble?' Mrs. White asked. She called the boys to catch the pig, and the game began.

"'Whee! You can't catch me!' Sassy Pants squealed with delight! With three little boys in hot pursuit, Sassy Pants chased around the house—under the table, into the living room, down the hall, and under the bed. A boy on both sides and one at the foot—there was no place for Sassy Pants to go. She was caught! Back into the box she went. The boys moved it to the furnace room and put chairs down sideways on the floor to keep the box from tipping over. Sassy Pants thought the game was so much fun she made up her mind to play it again.

"The next day she managed to tip her box over for a second time and find her way to the kitchen. This time during the pursuit she knocked over a bucket of mop water onto the kitchen floor. She dashed under the chair where the laundry basket sat. Over it went; the basket full of clean clothes lay on the floor, soaking up dirty water. Sassy Pants did not notice, nor did she care. She squealed at the sound of the crash and flew down the hall, wearing a pillowcase across her nose and a sock on her tail. She did look funny, but now an entire basket of fresh, clean clothes was dirty and wet. Mrs. White had to wash them again. She was not happy, not happy indeed, but Sassy Pants was. Jim, boy number two, caught her and gently put her back in her box. Life was good in the big house. Eat, sleep, play; eat, sleep, and play. Life could not be better; she felt like one of the family. While she slept, dreaming happy, little piggy sorts of dreams, the boys built a fence of chairs.

"The day after that, Sassy Pants was out of her box for a third time. This time she found it more difficult to wiggle out of the boys' fence. She also found that Mrs. White had put a chair in front of the door to make it difficult to open, but somehow Sassy Pants found a way. She was, after all, a determined little pig. She oinked and grunted contentedly as she greeted Mrs. White in the kitchen. 'Oh, no! You again, you sassy little pig! You better keep your pants in your box, or back to the pigpen with you!' she exclaimed. 'Boys, she is at it again!' Mrs. White called, and three little boys came running. The chase was on! What fun! 'You can't catch me!' Sassy Pants squealed and ran for the living room. Under the sewing machine she went. She did not notice, nor did she care that Mrs. White's sewing was now on the floor. She scooted behind the rocker on the slippery floor, bolted between the piano legs, out the other side, and smashed into the little table full of Mrs. White's favorite flowers. Dirt, water, and flowers were all over the floor, all over Sassy Pants, and some on the boys. She did not notice, nor did she care that she was making muddy hoof prints on the living room floor. Mrs. White swooped around the corner and snatched her up as she dashed from the living room to the hallway. 'That does it! Your sassy little pants are going back to the pigpen! If you are big enough to make that kind of mess, you are big enough to live in the pigpen and eat from the trough with the other pigs!' Back to the box she went until Farmer White came home. Tom, boy number three, put a lid on the box and wedged the door shut. After that, everyone called her Sassy Pants.

"Over supper, Farmer White heard the tale of Sassy Pants's escapade. A laugh wrinkle appeared at the corners of his eyes and a grin tugged at his mouth, but he agreed. The pig had to go. She no longer needed a bottle, and with all the good table scraps she had been eating, Sassy Pants had grown. The bigger she became, the bigger the mess she made—not that she noticed, nor that she cared. She was having fun; she was part of the family... or so she thought.

"In the morning, the sun came up as it always did. The rooster crowed to wake everyone as he always did, and Sassy Pants lay curled in her box as she always did, dreaming little piggy sorts of dreams. Suddenly, a pair of big, strong hands reached down and scooped her up. 'What? What? What? Hey! I'm sleeping here!' squealed Sassy Pants. Farmer White kept walking, with Sassy Pants under his arm. He was a determined man, you see, and no amount of squealing could make him stop. The next thing Sassy Pants knew, she was standing in the pigpen, blinking in the sun. 'There you go,' Farmer White said, swatting her little bum. 'Off to play with the rest of the piggies!'

"'What did he say?' she asked herself. 'Did he call me a pig? I am no pig! I am a people, part of the family!' She snorted with her tail in a curl and her snout in the air. 'I am special. I live in the big house, not the pigpen. I sleep on a blanket, not a bed of straw. I eat from a table, not a trough. I am a people, not a pig! In the big house I will be.' Sassy Pants snorted and stomped; she grunted and thought and thought some more. She thought of what was hers and what she was due. She thought herself into thinking far more highly of herself than she ought."

WELCOME BACK TO THE PIG PEN

"One of Sassy Pants's sisters ran squealing into the pig barn with the news! 'Farmer White brought Sassy Pants home!' There was a great deal of sniffing and snorting and squealing going on for a while as Mrs. Pig and her big family welcomed Sassy Pants home. Her poor mama was not sure what had happened to her, so she had to check Sassy out from top to bottom—and, yes, she was all there. Then Mrs. Pig had a little cry.

The relief was almost more than her poor nerves could take! Sassy Pants's brothers and sisters rolled and climbed all over her and each other; they were so happy to see her. Everyone talked at once. It was much noisier than Sassy Pants remembered, and in the shock of it all, she seemed quite quiet, almost shy. But that idea was soon corrected!

"Mrs. Pig soon realized that something else needed correcting also. Sassy Pants did not seem to know how to act like a pig, at least not in Mrs. Pig's eyes! She set right about teaching Sassy how to roll in the mud hole, how to eat at the pig trough in proper pig fashion, and how to rout for tasty roots and nuts. Sassy Pants drew back from the wallow as if to say, 'Eew! I am not going in there! That stuff *stinks!* You won't get *me* in *there!*' She did watch, however, to see how to do it—just out of curiosity, of course. Not that she was interested... or might want to try it, you see! And then there was the eating trough. She turned up her nose at the 'pig soup'—the left-over vegetables, week-old kitchen garbage, rotten cabbage and onions mixed with spoiled grain, and whey from the creamery where Farmer White sold his cream. Sassy Pants was horrified! Table scraps were one thing, but all this other stuff? And, eeeeew! The smell!

"Sassy Pants lived most unhappily with the pigs. She sighed deep sighs and felt sorry for herself. She chose to nap under the hickory nut tree and avoided the mud hole. She was not going to be a 'dirty pig.' She held off as long as she could, but after three days without food, she felt as though her tummy was rubbing her backbone! She was so hungry even the smelly things from the trough looked good. She chowed down with the rest of them and learned to dig with her snout for tasty roots and nuts.

"Finally, one hot day she could resist no longer and wallowed in the mud hole. All the while she complained to anyone who would listen of how Mrs. White banished her to the pigpen. As Sassy Pants became dirty and smelly like a pig, she also became angrier, sorrier for herself, and more determined by the day. She thought and thought and looked for ways to return to the big house. It was all she talked about, all she thought about. With all that angry thinking in her head, she began to think of mean, sneaky things she would do the minute she found a way out of the pen. She decided to get even with Mrs. White for putting her out of the house. The other pigs soon tired of all her fussing and all her talk; Sassy Pants was no fun to play with. They left her to herself. The more she talked to herself about her plight, the meaner Farmer and Mrs. White seemed to become."

THE ESCAPE

"One day while routing alone in the far corner of the pen, Sassy Pants's beady little eye spied a wee small hole under the fence. She studied and studied the hole. *Aha!* she thought. *If I make that hole a bit bigger, I can escape*. She began to dig.

"Wise Old Clyde and I stood watching from the other side of the fence. I was a rather timid little sheep back then," Miss Molly said. "I was so shy I had a hard time saying what I wanted to say, but Old Clyde never laughed or made fun of me. Old Clyde leaned his big head over the fence close to Sassy Pants's ear. 'I would not do that if I were you,' he said quietly. 'Farmer White makes fences for our protection.'

"'D-d-don't do it, Sassy Pants!' I stammered. 'There m-m-might be a c-c-coyote or a w-w-wolf or some big machine out there! Don't go out! Listen to what Old Clyde says. Farmer White wants to protect you, even if you don't believe it!' Sassy Pants took no notice, nor did she care what we or her other barnyard friends said. She threw more dirt out of the hole.

"'Fences keep trouble out,' Old Clyde commented, as a pile of dirt landed on his hoof."

Miss Molly leaned closer to the children and looked over her glasses. "But that, you see, that was it! Trouble was what Sassy Pants wanted *into,* not *out of!*

"She dug and dug, making the hole bigger and bigger. She was much larger now than she had been, but she continued to work, routing and routing. Finally, the hole was big enough; she pushed and shoved until she wiggled through. Of course, her underneath was covered with dirt from her pink, curly, little tail to her pushy little snout.

"Without so much as a 'Goodbye, it has been nice talking with you,' Sassy Pants went straight to the house and oinked at Mrs. White. 'Mrs. White!' she declared, 'I am going to live with you in the big house and eat table food. I am special—a part of the family.'

"Mrs. White looked out the door. 'Well, you dirty, sassy, little pig! What are you doing here? Back to the pigpen with you!' She dashed out the door to catch Sassy

Pants, who bolted and ran. Around and around the house they went. 'Boys!' called Mrs. White, flapping her apron. 'That ornery little pig is at it again.' Three little boys came running around the corner; old times were back again! But, no. They caught her and promptly put her back in the pig-pen. No one gave her a piggy treat, and no one scratched her ears or said she was cute.

"I am sorry to say, at that moment Sassy Pants made a very bad choice. 'Put me back in the pigpen, will they! Farmer and Mrs. White are mean to me, so I will be mean to them!' she said with her snout in the air and to no one in particular. Squinting her piggy little eyes, she made them look mean. At that moment, her piggy little heart became as hard as a stone!"

THE FATEFUL CHOICE

"The sun coming up was Sassy Pants's signal to escape quickly before anyone was awake. She wiggled out of the hole again and explored the barnyard before going to the big house. She was dirty from one end to the other. 'Oink, oink, oink. Snort, grunt, grunt,' she said. Mrs. White would have no part of a dirty, smelly pig; she did not invite Sassy Pants in. Now, Mrs. White had four boys, three little ones and one big one.

She called them right away and waved her apron to make Sassy Pants go back to the barnyard. Instead, around the house she went, straight into Mrs. White's garden. She dashed down a row of green beans, pulling them up as she went, which made Denny, the oldest and biggest of the four boys, very happy. He did not like green beans. Mrs. White was not happy, not happy indeed. 'Catch that sassy little troublemaking pig before she ruins the garden!' cried Mrs. White. 'You naughty, mean, little pig! Oh, I would shorten your tail right up next to your ears if I could catch you!' she called after the fleeing pig. The littlest boy, Dale George, jumped up from behind a rhubarb plant and grabbed Sassy Pants around the middle; but, I am sorry to say, she had already stomped her pointed little feet on enough tomatoes to make spaghetti sauce for a month! He had to hold her around the middle, you see, because pigs are round on one end and pointy on the other; but little boys can hold them by the middle!

"'Sassy Pants,' said Dale George, boy number four, to the wiggling piggy, 'you are making big trouble. The garden is no place for you. Everything in this garden we eat. You better stay where you belong!' I am sorry to say, she was beginning to look and smell more piggy by the day! She had dirt on her snout from routing in the field. She had dirt underneath from crawling under the fence. She had dirt on her top from rolling in the mud; but she did not notice, nor did she care. Dale George held her tight, as dirty and smelly as she was, until Jim and Tom made a rope halter to keep her from running away. Sassy Pants had grown so much bigger that the little boys could not carry her. She had to walk back to the pig-pen with two boys holding the rope. Dale George took a bath.

"'Humph,' said Sassy Pants. 'Mrs. White is mean! Tomorrow I *will* go again. She will be sorry she was mean to me!' The next day she watched and waited until Farmer White went to the field—she knew she had to make her escape when *he* was not around. True to her word, Sassy Pants wiggled out the hole and returned to the scene of the crime. She remembered the food in the garden. *If it is good for boys, it is good for pigs,* she thought. She did not greet Mrs. White. Visiting with her did not seem to be going well. She went straight to the garden—to the carrots, potatoes, and beans. She dug up potatoes and chomped down carrots; she ate onions and beans. She stepped on tomatoes and made hoof prints in cucumbers. She took a bite of cabbage and turned up her nose at rutabagas. About that time, Mrs. White came to pick beans for supper and found Sassy Pants with a beet hanging from her snout. The garden was in shambles.

"'Aaah, aaaagh, aaaagh!' was all Mrs. White could say. She ran after Sassy Pants, waving her apron and calling the boys. They came from four different directions, and for a moment, Sassy Pants did not move.

"'I got her; I got her!' yelled Tom, boy number three, as he made a dive. Sassy Pants jumped straight up in the air, whirled around, and flew like a shot—making a hole in the garden fence. She ran through the flowerbed and then the rose hedge. She did not notice the trouble she caused, nor did she care. She ran right back to the pigpen—since that was where she would go anyway.

Jim opened the gate, and in she walked as though she had done nothing wrong.

"'Trouble,' said Mrs. White. 'You are smart, and you are trouble. What am I to do for a garden now?' And so it went. Day after day, Sassy Pants found her way out of the pen and into trouble."

THE TROUBLESOME SUMMER

"Usually, summer on the northeast Iowa farm snuggled up against the state forest is a happy time filled with warm, sunny days, fun and games, and lazy afternoon naps under the shade trees. The memory of that summer still makes us older farm animals shudder. Sassy Pants became a barnyard bully! When she realized that Farmer White and his wife actually *wanted* her to live in the pigpen, Sassy Pants became grumpy and mean. She simply would not accept the decision. No, she was either going to be a part of the family and live in the big house or else. She began to terrorize the barnyard family and in that way, upset Farmer White.

"Oh!" said Miss Molly as she shuddered at the thought.

"Sassy Pants was such a pest that the little folk (the chickens and such) and us children of the barnyard asked the bigger animals for help. They said we should ask Georgia, head cow for the herd. She made all the decisions for the herd. She was good at making decisions. When she heard the stories, she immediately said, 'Well, you all need to talk with Mrs. Pig.' Off we went and told our stories to Mrs. Pig.

"Poor lady! She just sat down in a heap with tears running down her face. 'I am so sorry my child has been behaving in such a manner. I did not know all this was going on. I have my hooves more than full trying to manage a family of nineteen. I do not have the time to stop in at the barnyard listening post. Eighteen of my children are as well behaved as any pig can be; but I must tell you, I don't think my talking to Sassy Pants will have any effect. Since she came back to the pigpen after being in the big house, she will not listen to me. I am beside myself! My nerves are all frazzled. I have tried everything I can think of. I do not know what to do anymore! Maybe you should talk to Borus Hog.' And then she had another little cry. Everyone ran over to the pigpen and gathered by the gate to share their stories with Borus Hog in the hope that *he* could make Sassy Pants behave.

"Banty Rooster's wife, Beatrice, spoke first. 'After Farmer White went to the field,

Sassy Pants opened the door to the hen house, frightened all us hens and chickens, and chased us out into the barnyard. She laughed when we squawked and flew every which direction; then she yelled, "Bird brain, stupid chickens!" Banty Rooster came to our rescue, but Sassy Pants snapped her teeth together as if she were going to eat him. He flew up on the fence, out of her reach. 'What a bird brain!' Sassy Pants laughed. 'That will give you something to crow about, chicken liver!' The fracas upset us laying hens so badly we could not lay eggs for two days! Maude, the setting hen, became so nervous she could hardly keep her eggs warm. She clucked and fussed until Mrs. White moved her to a quiet place where Sassy Pants could not reach.'

"Kitty Cat chimed in. 'She frightened my babies and me and chased us under the corncrib. She taunted us and called us 'fraidy cats!' Little Thomas, one of my kittens, was so frightened he backed up under the corncrib too far; he became stuck and could not get out. That night when we came for milk, Dale George noticed that there was one kitten missing. Fortunately for us, Dale George was a little guy. He was able to crawl under the corncrib far enough to reach Little Thomas.'

"Martha, the top milking cow, said, 'Everyone is nervous because you never know who she is going to frighten or be mean to next. In fact, Sassy Pants's trouble-making has me in such a state, my milk is about to go sour. You can be sure that would not set well with Farmer White! The barnyard is in an uproar!'

Miss Molly again leaned forward to be close to the children. "My mother, Matilda

Merino, was a woman of few words, but when she talked, you listened. She shared that Sassy Pants was involved in some risky behavior. 'She purposefully rolls in the mud wallow, gets out through her hole, brushes up against the little lambs, and makes their wool dirty and smelly. We have to walk around with our children smelling like pigs until the dried mud falls off from walking through bushes. That little "joke" is particularly dangerous, you see, because lambs need to smell like their mothers, or the mothers think some stranger is trying to take their baby's lunch. A mamma sheep will refuse to feed her own lamb if he smells wrong! Sassy Pants may have thought her "joke" funny, but it could have deadly results. Fortunately, that has not happened; but Sassy Pants could cause the death of a lamb! This is serious behavior, and it *must* stop. All the ewes try to watch for her, but she sneaks up behind or catches us when we are not looking. It is awful; it is nerve racking!'

"'You can say that again, that again!' the twins, Darlene and Dominic Duck, chimed in. 'This young pig has ruffled our feathers to the point we are about to quack up!'

"Goosie Goose spoke next. 'She turned over our water trays and told us we didn't have sense enough to come in out of the rain. Doesn't she know we are water birds? We love to be wet! She really hurt my little goslings' feelings. Old Gander flew after her, beat her about the head with his big, strong wings, bit her ears, pecked her behind, and hissed at her. While running away Sassy Pants said, "Naaah, naaah, naaah, naaah nah! Didn't hurt!" However, later we noticed her looking sad, flicking her ears as if they still hurt, and soaking her behind in the mud hole.

"'Little Gerald Gosling Goose III stretched his fuzzy little neck to take a long look between the fence boards. He leaned against me and said, "Mommy, she looks like she's sorry."

"'To which I replied, "Well, son, there are two kinds of sorry: Sorry because you realize you hurt someone or did wrong, and then there is feeling sorry for yourself because you were caught and punished."

"'Gerald said, "Oh, which sorry do you think it is? She does not look very big right now. Her muscles are not any bigger than anyone else's. She does not look ferocious! Do you think when she is angry that it puffs her up? Can her anger make her look bigger, stronger, and meaner?"

"'I said, "Gerald, I think you may be right!" Anyhow, she has not bothered us since. Maybe that thrashing and pecking helps her remember her manners around my family!'

"Borus Hog nodded in agreement as he listened with a scowl on his face. In all the years Borus had been on the farm, no pig had ever behaved so badly—and Borus is older than dirt! First, Borus said, 'I would like to apologize for your distress and the trouble Sassy Pants is making.' Looking at my mother, he said, 'And I realize that smelling like a pig is not for everyone. Now, before I talk with Sassy Pants, I would like for you ladies, and all the dads, to have a talk with her. See if it helps to have the dads involved. If it does not, I *will* lay down the law. She may be one of those who chooses to learn the hard way rather than the easy way.'

"My mom asked Sir Reginald Ram to go with her," said Miss Molly. "Sir Reginald used all his wonderful logic and reasoning to point out the troubles Sassy Pants caused and carefully made sure she understood how this affected everyone. My mom thought Sassy Pants *had* to understand the consequences of her actions when Sir Reggie was finished. Surely, she would behave now! But Sir Reggie might as well have saved his breath!

"Fred the bull talked to her, but she just looked at him and said, 'Well, I guess that is your problem now, isn't it?' She turned and walked away with her snooty snout in the air. Fred's nostrils flared, but he controlled himself. He admitted that it took great restraint to keep from kicking 'that little pigskin right between the fence posts, right back into the pigpen!'

"Grey Tommy, Little Thomas's dad, tried to talk with her. She appeared to be listening politely but then suddenly jumped at Grey Tommy and made a snorty noise. Grey Tommy went straight up in the air and then straight up the barnyard light pole. Sassy Pants rolled on the ground in laughter. 'Scaredy cat!' she taunted and staggered off laughing. Nobody else thought it was funny. Grey Tommy said that little episode scared him out of three of his nine lives!

"One of the nanny goats asked Billy Goat to butt heads with Sassy Pants. If talking, logic, and reasoning would not work, maybe he could *push* some sense into her and she could see the error of her ways. But no, even that made no difference.

"That did it; Borus Hog *had* to lay down the law. First, he had to clear up one thing. 'Sassy Pants,' he said, 'in spite of what you think, you *are* a pig!' Then he stated the rules very clearly. 'Here are the rules all pigs live by.

1. Pigs of all sizes and shapes live in the pigpen and sleep in the pig barn on straw. Pigs wallow in the mud and eat from the trough.
2. Fences are for protection. Do not go outside the fence.
3. Respect others, even if they are different from you. They may not look like you or sound like you. They may not be as brave or as strong as you are, but you respect them.
4. Say "please" and "thank you."

5. Greet everyone politely, and say "good-bye" when you leave.
6. You may play with Farmer White's children, as long as you stay *in* the pigpen.
7. When you play with other animals, play fair and be kind. No bullying. No name-calling.
8. Do not scare someone for the fun of it. It is not funny.

"'Am I clear? Do you understand? I will talk with Farmer White; if you break the rules, there will be consequences. You will not like them.

"When Borus Hog finished with the Laws of the Pigpen, there was a moment when Sassy Pants had to admit to herself that what she was doing really did not make sense. Nobody liked her or wanted to play with her anymore. She did not know what made her owly and growly or why she did the mean things she did. However, she did not let those thoughts stay around very long. She snorted and walked away with an attitude that said she could not be bothered with all Mr. Hog's rules and being 'nicey nice'! She was not going to listen or care what anyone thought—not even the top hog! Mr. Hog shook his head. This young lady was a case! He waited for Farmer White to come in from the field. They had a talk. Mr. Hog never told us what he and Farmer White discussed.

"Like clockwork, Sassy Pants escaped again, in spite of what Mr. Hog said. She ate her fill of the nuts the boys had gathered and laid out in the grass by the side of the barnyard driveway to dry in the sun. After she finished eating, she scattered the rest all over the ground. In the wintertime, all four boys liked to sit by the fire and crack the nuts and pick the nutmeats out for Mrs. White to put into cookies—if there were any left they did not eat! When the boys found the mess she made, they did not think it very funny. And so it went, all summer long; every chance she had, Sassy Pants upset the barnyard animals and made trouble to pester Farmer White. Every chance she had, she broke into Mrs. White's garden to give her fits. Sassy Pants took no notice, nor did she care that everyone in the barnyard and out of it had their feathers ruffled or their fur in a knot! Mrs. White put the boys to work looking for Sassy Pants's hole. They looked and looked, but they could not find it. The mischief continued. Everyone was a nervous wreck! It seemed the whole summer would be a disaster.

"Finally, Farmer White found the hole, and he fixed it. He fixed it good. Sassy Pants would *never* get out there again. He put down the big 16 pound mall that he used to pound the post in the ground and stood looking at her. She pretended to rout in the dirt like all the other pigs, as though she did not notice or care. All the while, she carefully kept one eye on Farmer White and his big, strong hands. 'Troublesome pig, troublesome,' he said. 'We can't have troublesome pigs.'

"Sassy Pants heard what he said, but I am sorry to say, she made another very bad choice. Instead of choosing to be happy routing in the dirt and rolling in the mud, she threw a little fit and wanted people things. Instead of saying 'thank you' for the food Farmer White gave her every day, she longed for table scraps, games with little boys, and a box with a blanket. She wanted things she could not have; she nearly made herself sick! Then she made *the* decision—she was not just going to pester Farmer White, she was going to make him pay for making her stay in the pigpen! She was better than all these 'dirty pigs'! She would get even with Farmer White! So Sassy Pants tried and tried to break out, with no success. She huffed and puffed. 'I'll have to find another way,' she said."

THE LAST STRAW

"Days went by without any trouble. Sassy Pants had accepted living in the pigpen—so it *seemed*. Everyone began to relax. We thought life was back to normal. One evening as Farmer White fed the pigs, Sassy Pants studied the gate where he came in. After he left, she tried to open it. She pushed and she shoved, but it would not open. She tried to lift the latch, but it was too high. Tired from trying, she leaned on the gate—it moved! She leaned again, harder. It opened wider, but Farmer White was still nearby. The escape would have to wait until morning. Sassy Pants, squinting her beady little eyes, allowed her hard little heart to grow harder still. She began to plan the mean, naughty thing she would do—how she would make Farmer White pay. He would be sorry, sorry indeed for making her stay in the pigpen. She went to sleep with a mean, nasty little grin on her face. It was a very bad choice she made, as you will see.

"In the morning, Sassy Pants waited until Farmer White did all the barnyard chores, put the cows out to pasture, and went to the field. She leaned on the pigpen gate, harder and harder, until it opened wide enough to slip through. She knew right where to go—through the barnyard, across the lawn, and up on the porch where Farmer White kept his can of cream in a big tub of cold water until the milkman came to take it to market. Sassy Pants put her hard little snout under the tub; over it went, crashing to the porch. The cream can lid came off and cream poured out. Sassy Pants drank all she could drink. It felt good on the inside of her tummy, so it should feel good on the outside! Cream was supposed to be good for the skin, she had heard someone say. Sassy Pants began to bathe in the cream. She lay on her tummy and then rolled to her back. She wiggled this way and that, making a magnificent mess. Sassy Pants did not notice, nor did she care. The cream felt glorious!

"Suddenly, the house door opened. There stood Mrs. White with a horrible look on her face. She called for Denny, the biggest boy of them all, to help with 'this pig.' Mrs. White was so angry she did not even call Sassy Pants by name. She called her 'this pig.'"

Miss Molly's face became serious and concerned. "You see," she continued, "Farmer White sold the cream to buy flour and sugar and cereal and clothing for the children. Now there would be no money to buy those things. This happened back in 1950. The war was over, but people in this part of Iowa still had to be very careful about how they spent their money. There was not a whole lot extra! It was very mean and naughty of Sassy Pants to spill the cream all over the ground and then bathe in it!

"It took four boys to catch one slippery, muddy, cream-covered pig; but catch her they did. They marched her to the pigpen, wired the gate shut, and then they all took a bath in the creek. When Farmer White heard about the cream, his face became stormy and serious. 'That is the last straw. You have really done it now, pig,' he said, shaking his head as he looked at her over the fence. 'You have really done it now. We will not have a troublesome pig on this farm.'

"Farmer White turned and went to the barnyard light pole. He did something, but Sassy Pants could not quite see what it was. She pretended not to be watching. She pretended to rout in the leaves and act like she was looking for tasty roots, but she was really trying to see what Farmer White was doing. It might give her a clue for another way out."

SOME LEARN THE HARD WAY

"Old Clyde and Martha the cow stood under the shade of the old hickory nut tree. Every year that tree dropped bushels of nuts for the pigs to eat. Old Clyde blinked big, sleepy eyes and swatted flies with his tail. He stood close to Martha. Two days earlier, Sassy Pants chewed the long curl off the end of Martha's tail. There was no lovely long hair to swish flies; only a club to clobber them! Old Clyde swished to the right over Martha's back and then to the left over his own back. Martha burped up a big, particularly delicious cud of grass and chewed blissfully. It felt good to relax—with Sassy Pants in view it was safe to relax. 'Do you think we should tell her about the electric fence?' asked Martha.

"Old Clyde studied Sassy Pants for a long time and then shook his head. 'No, I don't think so. She would not believe us. She would think we were just trying to scare her into staying inside the fence. No, I think she needs to learn that fences are there for a good reason. She needs to learn to respect them, even if she does not like them, even if she does not believe they are for her own good. Some folks learn the easy way, and some learn the hard way. Best leave her be.'

"Now, hickory nuts are like chocolates for pigs—irresistible. Porketta, Sassy Pants's big sister, was eating nuts like there would not be any left tomorrow. With her mouth full, she called to Sassy Pants, 'Hey, Sassy! *Smack, smack.* The nuts are great! Come have some! *Smack, smack.*' But this day, Sassy Pants had no time for hickory nuts. She walked right on by, kicking nuts this way and that. Porketta could not believe her eyes!

"Sassy Pants had decided that today was the day. She had to get out of that pen. The summer was nearly over; it was not right for her still to be in a pigpen—she was a people, not a pig…or so she thought, in spite of what Borus Hog said. Soon, Old Clyde and Martha watched her curly little tail disappear down the hill. Sassy Pants was going to check every last inch of the fence. If there was even a tiny hole, she would make it bigger, and out she would go. She was sure she could find one—she *had* to find one!

"Down the hill she went, turned the corner, and walked alongside the creek. Not a hole to be seen. Back up the hill on the other side she went, testing the wire to see if she could create a hole where there was none. Sassy Pants was going to either go uphill or downhill no matter where she went. That's the way this farm is—up or down, all of it! Finally, at the far corner on the far side of the pen, she found what she was looking for. The first hole she made that Farmer White fixed was a little beyond. This was a place where the rain washed the dirt away from the fence. It was not very big, but it had promise! And there was only one thin wire across the washout. This was going to be easy!

"Sassy Pants knew she had found her escape route! She would test it to see how much bigger she needed to make the hole. Wonderful, wonderful! It was enough out of sight that she was confident she could get away without anyone being the wiser. She marched right up to that wire and reached out with her tough little snout to give it a good push.

"Farmer White did the evening chores. He fed and watered the sheep, the calves and the pigs, and now he sat milking the cows. Suddenly there was a frightful squealing and carrying on coming from the pigpen. Farmer White did not move a muscle to go see what the matter was. But a slow grin started on one side of his face and worked its way around to the other. 'Some learn the easy way, and some learn the hard way,' he said to no one in particular and kept right on milking.

"Old Clyde and Martha the cow heard the ruckus too. 'Oh,' said Old Clyde with a sympathetic look, 'that has to smart!'

"'Yes,' Martha agreed, 'but like you said, she would not listen. Some do have to learn the hard way.' They shook their heads and stomped their feet and swished their tails to make the flies go away. 'I'm sure she will be a different pig now,' Martha said. Old Clyde had to agree.

"Sassy Pants's snout had no more than touched that thin wire when a jolt went from her snout, through her body, and right out her tail. She saw bright lights and sparkles. Her ears were ringing. She squealed; she snorted and made all sorts of strange noises—she could not talk right or walk right. When she finally could see without spots in front of her eyes, she began to check herself out. Her snout was throbbing. It was probably going to be swollen like the time a bee stung her, but *that* was no bee! She turned to look at her tail—her curly, pink little tail that she was so proud of! She gasped. It wasn't curly! She looked closer. 'Oh! No!' she exclaimed. The sandy tufts of hair on the end of her tail were singed black.

"Now, if you had glasses that would let you see high-falutin ideas and bad behaviors, you would have seen them flying all over the place. The shock from that electric fence blew every fancy, better-than-you idea and mean thought right out of Sassy Pants's head! She stood there for a while, shaking her head to make the sparkles go away. Then she walked a kind of sideways, funny sort of walk over to the mud hole and flopped down in the mud. It was cool. It felt wonderful on her throbbing snout.

"A big mud bubble formed, eyes appeared above the mud, and big brother Bruno asked, 'Hey, Sassy Pants! What was all that noise about?'

"Sassy Pants was uncharacteristically quiet. Finally, she blew a bubble in the mud and said, somewhat sullenly, 'I don't want to talk about it.' Not that day anyway.

"Little by little, the story leaked out and word passed around the barnyard. Sassy Pants was a reformed pig—she noticed, and she cared!"

listen|imagine|view|experience

AUDIO BOOK DOWNLOAD INCLUDED WITH THIS BOOK!

In your hands you hold a complete digital entertainment package. Besides purchasing the paper version of this book, this book includes a free download of the audio version of this book. Simply use the code listed below when visiting our website. Once downloaded to your computer, you can listen to the book through your computer's speakers, burn it to an audio CD or save the file to your portable music device (such as Apple's popular iPod) and listen on the go!

How to get your free audio book digital download:

1. Visit www.tatepublishing.com and click on the e|LIVE logo on the home page.
2. Enter the following coupon code:
   898d-ab66-ec26-eee0-131d-2c17-7ddb-e660
3. Download the audio book from your e|LIVE digital locker and begin enjoying your new digital entertainment package today!